WELCOME TO

HAWAI'I VOLCANOES

NATIONAL PARK

BY TERI AND BOB TEMPLE

MAP KEY

The maps throughout this
book use the following icons:

 Driving Excursion

 Hiking Trail

 Lodging

 Nēnē Viewing Area

 Overlook

 Picnic Area

 Point of Interest

 Ranger Station

 Visitor Center

 Wooded Area

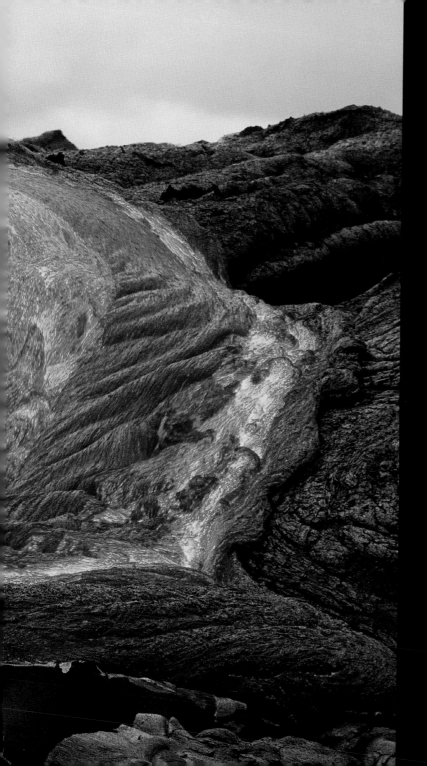

About National Parks

A national park is an area of land that has been set aside by Congress. National parks protect nature and history. In most cases, no hunting, grazing, or farming is allowed. The first national park in the United States—and in the world—was Yellowstone National Park. It is located in parts of Wyoming, Idaho, and Montana. It was founded in 1872. In 1916, the U.S. National Park Service began.

Today, the National Park Service manages more than 415 sites. Some of these sites are historic, such as the Statue of Liberty or the Martin Luther King Jr. National Historic Site. Other park areas preserve wild land. The National Park Service manages 40% of the nation's wilderness areas, including national parks. Each year, millions of people from around the world visit these national parks. Visitors may camp, go canoeing, or go for a hike. Or, they may simply sit and enjoy the scenery, wildlife, and the quiet of the land.

TABLE OF

The Child's World®
childsworld.com

Published by The Child's World®
1980 Lookout Drive
Mankato, MN 56003-1705
800-599-READ • www.childsworld.com

ISBN
9781503823433

LCCN
2017944778

Cartographer
Matt Kania/Map Hero, Inc.

Photo Credits
Alexander Demyanenko/Shutterstock.com: 21; Alexey Kamenskiy/
Shutterstock.com: 6-7; AZ68/iStockphoto.com: 1; Bettmann/Getty: 16;
Christian Weber/Shutterstock.com: 10; Everett Historical/Shutterstock.com:
20; George Burba/Shutterstock.com: 14; Historical Picture Archive/Getty:
17; Ingo70/Shutterstock.com: 23; National Geographic Creative/Alamy
Stock Photo: 24; National Park Service/Hawai'i Volcanoes National Park:
18; Nikki Gensert/Shutterstock.com: 26; Nathaniel Dance-Holland-from the
National Maritime Museum, United Kingdom/Public Domain: 19; OAR/
National Undersea Research Program (NURP); Univ. of Hawaii-Manoa: 27;
Ralf Broskvar/Shutterstock.com: 15; Tory Kallman/Shutterstock.com: 8-9;
USGS/Alamy Stock Photo: 13; Willyam Bradberry/Shutterstock.com: cover,
4; www.sandatlas.org/Shutterstock.com; 2-3

On the cover and this page
Hot lava creeps along at sunset. As lava cools,
it turns black.

On page 1
If you are lucky, you might see Kilauea shoot
lava high into the air.

On pages 2–3
Pu'u 'Ō'ō is one of Kilauea's eastern craters.
Lava flowing from Pu'u 'Ō'ō often flows through
underground tubes to the ocean.

Printed in the United States of America
PA02357

WELCOME TO HAWAIʻI VOLCANOES NATIONAL PARK

Λ

CONTENTS

🚶‍♂️🚶

Aloha!

HAWAI'I

Hawai'i Volcanoes National Park

Welcome to Hawai'i Volcanoes National Park! Here you can see two of the world's most active volcanoes. The park is located on the island of Hawai'i. It is part of the most **isolated** chain of islands in the world. In fact, Hawai'i is more than 2,000 miles (3,219 km) away from its nearest neighbor.

Visitors can see many different land types. Enjoy the green tree ferns of the rain forest. See the cold and snowy rock **summit** of a volcano. Feel the ocean breeze as you walk along the coast. Discover the centuries-old **fossilized** footprints of men, women, and children as you hike through the hot, dry desert. Wherever you go, you are bound to see some amazing things. There are plants and animals living in this park that are found nowhere else on Earth. Let's go explore the wonders of Hawai'i Volcanoes National Park!

In some areas, the park's rich soil, warm weather, and heavy rainfall make it the perfect home for thousands of types of plants and trees.

NATIONA

Safety First!

Hawai'i Volcanoes National Park is full of many natural wonders. Active volcanoes are interesting, but there are some **hazards** you won't find in other national parks. Here is a list for you to follow that puts safety first on your visit to this national park!

1. Drink a lot of water and use sunscreen. Prepare for all kinds of weather!
2. Volcanic gas is smelly and dangerous. Avoid the fumes!
3. Stay on the marked trails. Trees and bushes might be hiding a dangerous crack.
4. Stay back from the steep cliffs of the craters.
5. If you visit the coastal beaches, don't go swimming. Coastal beaches can be unsafe since the shores are rocky and the waves can be strong. Only swim in approved areas.

Hawaiian monk seals are very rare and are found only around the Hawaiian islands. Adult monk seals weigh about 400 pounds (181 kg) and are about seven feet (2 m) long. The seals get their name from the short hairs on their heads, which look a little like the hairstyle of long-ago monks.

Unique Life Zones

This area of Hawai'i is special. It has seven very different life zones. A life zone is an area of land that has its own special plants and animals. Hawai'i Volcanoes National Park takes you all the way from the coast to the tops of tall mountains. It runs through lively rain forests and across **barren** deserts. The weather is as different as the land.

Because of the park's **unique** landscape and location, a special ecosystem has developed over time. Hawai'i is like its own little world. All of the bugs, birds, and animals had to get here somehow. Some flew, like the hoary bat. Some swam, like the monk seal. These are the only two native mammals in Hawai'i. Birds carried some plants and other animals here. Others were blown along by the wind.

The Nēnē, or Hawaiian Goose

The nēnē is the state bird of Hawai'i. It looks a little like its closest relative, the Canada goose. The nēnē has short wings and long legs, and can often be seen walking in the park. It began to lose its **habitat** as Hawai'i changed. By the 1940s, there were only 50 nēnē birds left in the wild.

Hawai'i Volcanoes National Park began a project in the 1970s to protect the nēnē's habitat. That allowed the nēnē population to grow. It is working! Now there are close to 2,500 nēnē in the Hawaiian Islands. Maybe you can catch a glimpse of this beautiful **endangered** bird on your visit.

Active Volcanoes

What makes Hawai'i Volcanoes National Park so special? The volcanoes, of course! Here you can visit two of the world's most amazing volcanoes.

The first volcano is the giant Mauna Loa, the biggest mountain in the world. Most mountains tower over the earth. Mauna Loa is different. Most of this 56,000-foot (17,069 m) volcano is below the blue waves of the Pacific Ocean. Only 13,677 feet (4,169 m) of the mountain is above water.

The hike to the top of Mauna Loa is only for experienced hikers, but the sights you will see are amazing. On the trail to the summit are oddly shaped cinder cones. Hikers might even catch sight of a big-eyed hunting spider waiting for a fly or moth to blow by.

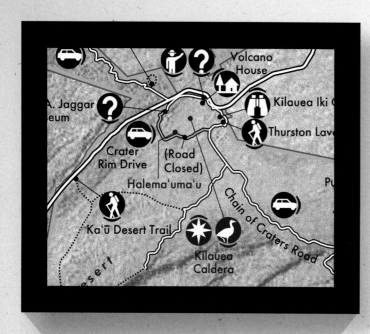

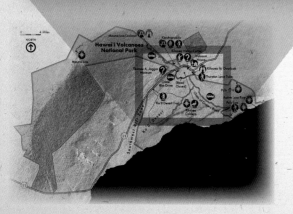

The main attraction of Hawai'i Volcanoes National Park is Kīlauea. It is only 4,000 feet (1,219 m) high, but it is the most active volcano in the world. Kīlauea's **caldera**, the large crater at the summit of the volcano, is more than 3 miles (5 km) wide and 400 feet (123 m) deep. Steam seeps out of rocks. The sulphur smell of **brimstone** fills the air. It looks and smells like another world!

A huge pit crater lies within Kīlauea's caldera. It is called Halema'uma'u. It began as a lava lake. In and around the volcano are rivers of cooled lava and steaming lava lakes.

You might think nothing could live in this hot, rocky landscape. Not true! Within the flowing lava, you can find tiny islands of land. A small universe of plants and animals can be found growing there. These islands are called kīpuka. The hapu'u, a tree fern, and the 'apapane, a native bird, thrive in these Hawaiian kīpuka.

This picture shows Halemaʻumaʻu (center), in Kilauea's caldera. The edges of Kilauea's caldera are spotted with huge boulders (some weighing as much as small cars) that were shot out of the earth by earlier eruptions.

The Legend of Pele

Hawaiian stories say that Kīlauea is the home of Pele, the goddess of fire. The story tells how Pele traveled from island to island. She searched for a home for her family and fire. Her sister, Nā-maka-o-kahaʻi, the goddess of the ocean, was chasing Pele. She destroyed every home Pele made. Pele finally found a safe home in Halemaʻumaʻu, the crater deep within Kīlauea.

Hawaiians have respected Pele's power ever since. People even leave offerings for her, but this isn't recommended as it can cause problems for wildlife. When visiting the park, you can help protect the park by leaving everything in its rightful place. At Kīlauea, where the very ground is **sacred** to the Hawaiian people, remember to e nihi ka hele, or walk softly.

Tree Molds and Lava Trees

There are all sorts of odd sights to see in the steamy, lava-flowing world of volcanoes. Among the unusual sights are lava trees and tree molds. Lava trees are made when hot lava cools around the trunk of a tree. As it cools, the lava becomes solid around the tree. Sometimes, the lava is so hot, the tree burns up. Then, a tree-shaped hole is left in the lava. This is called a tree mold. You can see these odd-shaped "trees" of lava all around the park.

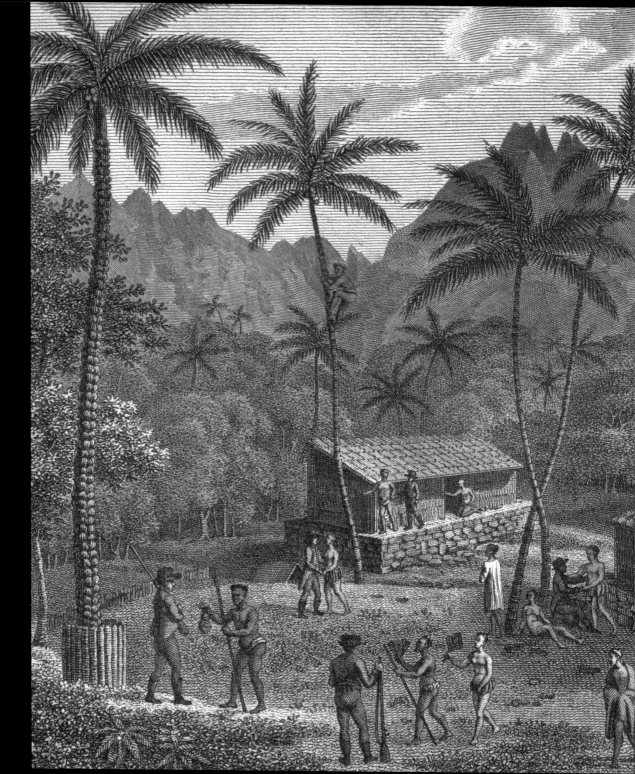

This drawing shows what life was like on the Marquesas Islands about 300 years ago. At that time, European and American explorers were arriving on the islands, causing many of the natives to become sick with diseases the visitors carried. Many natives were also captured and sold as slaves.

Opposite page: This small canoe is much like the larger ones early Polynesians used to journey to the Hawaiian islands.

Arrival of the Polynesians

Polynesians were the first settlers of the Hawaiian islands. They came from the Marquesas Islands to Hawai'i more than 1,600 years ago. People from the Society Islands also ventured to Hawai'i. Their journey took them over 2,400 miles (3,862 km) across the Pacific Ocean. They made the trip in sailing canoes.

Footprints in the Sand

In 1919, a scientist named Ruy H. Finch made an amazing discovery. Fossils of human footprints were found in the Kaʻū desert. Who made these ancient footprints? Scientists believe they were made by Hawaiian men, women, and children who were walking through the desert when Kilauea would erupt. The footprints were made more than several hundred years before 1790. The volcanic ash trapped the footprints, so we can still see them today.

These travelers brought with them many of the things they needed to survive. They introduced the puaʻa (pig), the ʻilio (dog), and the maiʻa (banana). After a while, because of the distance from their homeland, they were left alone. Soon, a new Hawaiian culture formed.

These village people were ruled by chiefs. They fished, raised crops, and recorded their stories in mele (song) and hula (dance). You can experience the Hawaiian culture at park festivals, cultural workshops, visitor demonstrations, and hotel lūʻau.

After humans arrived, the environment of Hawaiʻi changed. In 1778, a sea captain named James Cook happened upon the islands, and word of the discovery spread. Scientists soon came to the islands. They wanted to explore the great volcanoes.

James Cook (1728–1779) was a British sea captain, explorer, and mapmaker. He is best known for his discovery of the Hawaiian islands, but he was also the first person to sail the eastern coast of Australia as well as completely around New Zealand's islands.

19

A National Park

Typically the volcanoes in Hawai'i have more gentle eruptions than most volcanoes. As a result, they are safer to get close to and observe. Hawaiians came to the volcanoes to pay their respects to Pele. Others came when they heard about the amazing sights they might see. Two men, more than any others, helped turn the area into a national park.

Lorrin Thurston, a publisher, loved to explore the volcanoes. He tried to get people to understand how important they were. Thurston wanted to protect the volcanoes and the plants and animals that lived there. He had trouble getting that accomplished. Finally, he got some help from Dr. Thomas Jaggar.

In 1912, Thurston and Dr. Jaggar began to work together. They talked to people in government about the natural wonders of the land. They explained that scientists could learn a lot by studying the area. In 1916, their dream to make it a national park came true. President Woodrow Wilson made Hawai'i Volcanoes the 15th national park in America. Amazingly enough, Hawai'i wasn't even a state yet!

Thomas Woodrow Wilson (1856–1924) was the 28th president of the United States.

The Thurston Lava Tube

One of the most amazing things you will see in the park is a lava tube. A lava tube is created when a river of hot lava flows across the land. It forms a hard tube as the lava cools over a hot center. Eventually, all of the lava drains out of the center of the tube. This leaves a tunnel made of lava. One such tube, called the Thurston Lava Tube, is so large that you can actually walk through it when you explore Kilauea.

Crater Rim Drive

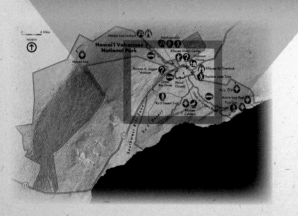

Hawai'i Volcanoes National Park is large. Still, you can explore much of it in just one day. So pack your backpack, jump in your car, and come explore the park. Let's start at the Kīlauea Visitor Center. There, you can learn about volcanoes and choose your route.

Crater Rim Drive is the main route. It takes you around parts of the Kīlauea Caldera. Some parts of the road are closed because of eruptions. Along this drive you can see the Volcano House. It was the first lodging on the mountain. Or, you can visit the Thomas A. Jaggar Museum. These places have some of the best views in the entire park.

Hike and drive along the rim. You can see steam and sulfur vents, pit craters, and lava flows from as recently as 1982. You can even walk through the misty rain forests. Or, take a stroll through a real lava tube!

Visitors can get a close-up view of this steam vent along Crater Rim Drive. Steam vents occur when moisture trickles down through cracks and holes in the ground. When the moisture reaches the volcano's hot lava rocks, it turns into steam.

Black Beaches

Have you ever seen a beach made of black sand? You can see them here at the park. They are created when hot lava from a volcano meets the cold water of the ocean. The cooled, black lava breaks into a million little pieces. These pieces travel in the water and eventually find a quiet spot on the shore. A black beach is born!

Amazing Sights

The Chain of Craters Road is full of amazing sights. It is 40 miles (64 km) round-trip. You might see red lava flowing from an eruption that started in 1983 and is still going today. Hike out to the Pu'u Loa Petroglyph Field to see the ancient symbols carved in lava. Feel the power of the ocean. Admire the island's newest black beaches.

Don't forget Mauna Loa. No trip would be complete without a visit to this sleeping giant. The road to Mauna Loa Overlook, at 6,662 feet (2,031 m), is windy and steep, but it is worth your effort. Along the way, you will be amazed by tree molds. Relax in a peaceful koa forest at Kīpukapuaulu and watch out for the big and beautiful Hawaiian dragonfly!

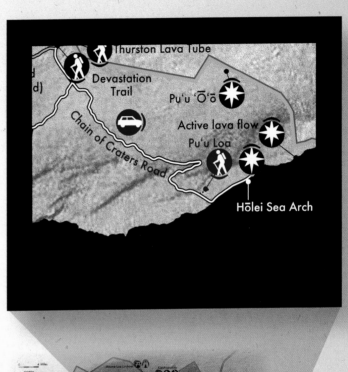

Pu'u Loa Petroglyph Field

Pu'u Loa means "hill of long life" in Hawaiian. Pu'u Loa Petroglyph Field is located on the southeast side of Kīlauea. It is a sacred place to Hawaiians. Here you will see symbols that were etched in the hard lava. These symbols are called petroglyphs.

Scientists believe that people from long ago carved these symbols. They wanted to tell others about their journeys and their daily lives. If you look closely, you might see a canoe, a person, or a fish! Take a walk and see if you can guess what the ancient Hawaiians had to say. Stay on the boardwalk and be careful not to step on the petroglyphs!

New Little Sister

There is a new volcano in town. It has been named Lōʻihi. The little sister of Kīlauea and Mauna Loa, it is the newest underwater active volcano. Lōʻihi is located about 20 miles (32 km) off the coast of the island of Hawaiʻi. It may well some day become the next island in the Hawaiian chain of islands.

Don't get too excited to visit her just yet. Lōʻihi is about 3,000 feet (914 m) under the ocean. If she continues to grow as fast as her sisters, we can expect to see her above the waves in about 60,000 years.

Day or night, any season at all, Hawaiʻi Volcanoes National Park is a place full of life and adventure. So come and explore the great volcanoes of Hawaiʻi!

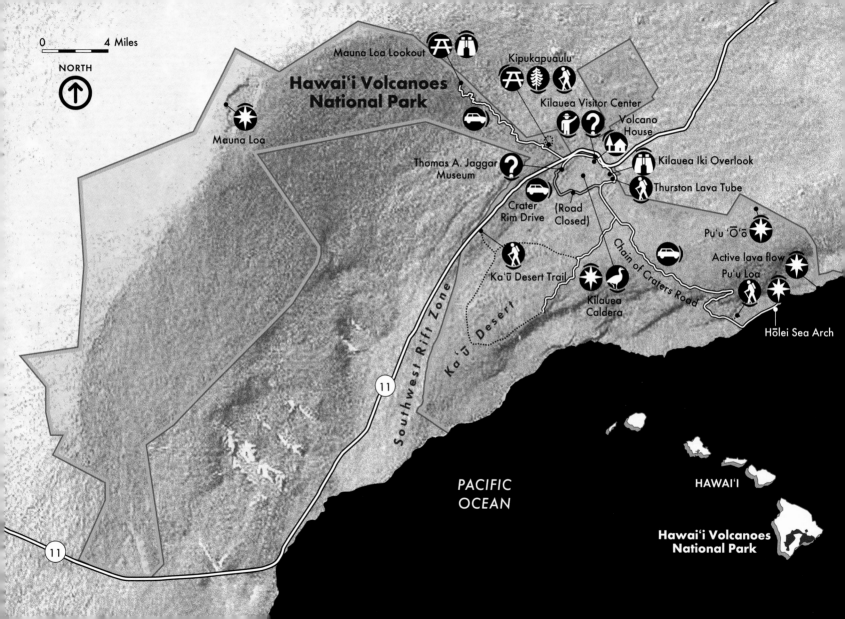

0   4 Miles

NORTH

Mauna Loa Lookout

Hawai'i Volcanoes National Park

Kipukapuaulu

Kilauea Visitor Center

Volcano House

Mauna Loa

Thomas A. Jaggar Museum

Kilauea Iki Overlook

Thurston Lava Tube

Crater Rim Drive

(Road Closed)

Pu'u 'Ō'ō

Active lava flow

Ka'ū Desert Trail

Chain of Craters Road

Pu'u Loa

Southwest Rift Zone

Ka'ū Desert

Kilauea Caldera

Hōlei Sea Arch

11

PACIFIC OCEAN

HAWAI'I

11

Hawai'i Volcanoes National Park

HAWAI'I VOLCANOES NATIONAL PARK FAST FACTS

Date founded: August 1, 1916

Location: In the state of Hawai'i, on the island of Hawai'i

Size: 505 square miles (1,308 sq km); 323,200 acres (130,794 hectares)

Major habitats: Seven distinct ecosystems—seacoast, lowland, mid-elevation woodland, rain forest, upland forest, subalpine, and alpine

Important landforms: Two active volcanoes, two calderas (craters), pit craters, cinder cones, tree molds, and rivers of lava

Elevation:
Highest: 13,677 feet (4,169 m) at Mauna Loa's summit
Lowest: Sea level

Weather:
Average yearly rainfall: 100 inches (254 cm) in the rain forest and less than 30 inches (76 cm) in the park's desert
Average temperatures: 84 F (29 C) to 69 F (21 C)
Highest: 88 F (31 C) in 1979
Lowest: 63 F (17 C) in 1955

Native animal species: Only two native mammals—hoary bat and Hawaiian monk seal

Main animal species: Nēnē (Hawaiian goose), Hawaiian hoary bat, Hawaiian monk seal, green sea turtle, hawksbill turtle, 'io (Hawai'i hawk), pueo (Hawaiian owl), 'apapane, 'amakihi, and 'i'iwi (3 kinds of honeycreeper birds), white-tailed tropicbird, Kamehameha butterfly

Number of plant species: More than 4,600 non-native species, 1,700 species native to Hawai'i (90% of those now extinct)

Main native plant species: 'Ōhi'a lehua tree, koa tree, tree fern (hapu'u), 'ohelo, 'a'ali'i, and pukiawe (three common shrubs), Mauna Loa silversword ('āhinahina). Most of the flowers associated with Hawai'i were imported.

Number of endangered animal/plant species: Six— Mauna Loa silversword, hoary bat, Hawaiian monk seal, nēnē (Hawaiian goose), hawksbill turtle, and Hawaiian petrel

Native people: Polynesians from the Marquesas and Society Islands

Number of visitors each year: About 2 million

Important sites and landmarks: Kīlauea Visitor Center, Sulphur Banks, Steaming Bluff, Jaggar Museum, Southwest Rift Zone, Halema'uma'u and Keanakāko'i Craters, Thurston Lava Tube, Kīlauea Iki Overlook, and Kīlauea Iki Crater

Tourist activities: Ranger-led nature walks and talks, visitor center movies, museum exhibits, hiking, bird watching, biking, camping, and photography

GLOSSARY

barren (BAYR-ren): A bare landscape is called barren. Lava from Hawaiian volcanoes flowed across the barren rocks.

brimstone (BRIM-stohn): Brimstone is an old-fashioned word for sulfur. The brimstone around the volcanoes smells like rotten eggs.

caldera (kal-DAYR-uh): A caldera is a crater that is made when lava drained from an underground lava chamber, causing the volcano summit to collapse. Kīlauea's caldera is more than 3 miles (5 km) wide.

endangered (en-DAYN-jurd): A living thing is endangered when it is in danger of becoming extinct. Hawai'i has the greatest number of endangered plants and animals in the world.

fossilized (FOSS-uh-lyzd): When something has been fossilized, it has become a fossil. A fossil is the remains or imprint of a prehistoric plant or animal. Scientists have found fossilized footprints near the volcanoes in Hawai'i Volcanoes National Park.

habitat (HAB-uh-tat): A habitat is the natural home, or environment, of a plant or animal. In Hawai'i Volcanoes National Park, the rain forest is the habitat for many birds.

hazards (HAZ-urdz): A hazard is a danger or risk. Be sure to look out for any hazards when exploring volcanoes.

isolated (EYE-soh-lay-ted): When something is set apart from others or alone, it is isolated. Hawai'i is isolated from the rest of the world.

sacred (SAY-kred): A symbol or part of a religious ceremony that is holy is called sacred. Some Hawaiians believe the volcanoes are sacred.

summit (SUM-mit): A summit is the highest point, or peak, of a mountain. It can be freezing on the summit of Mauna Loa.

unique (yoo-NEEK): When something is unique, it is one-of-a-kind. The lankdscape of Hawai'i Volcanoes National Park is unique.

Hawaiian Vocabulary

aloha (ah-loh-hah): Aloha means hello or goodbye. Make sure you say aloha to the park rangers.

hula (hoo-lah): Hula means dance in Hawaiian. You can see beautiful girls and handsome men dance the hula at a park cultural festival or hotel lūʻau.

ʻīlio (EE-lee-oh): ʻĪlio means dog in Hawaiian. ʻĪlio were brought to Hawaiʻi a long time ago by the Polynesians.

Kīlauea (KEE-lau-way-ah): Kīlauea means spewing or much spraying in Hawaiian. Kīlauea is also the name of the most active volcano in the world.

kīpuka (KEE-poo-kah): A kīpuka is an isolated island of land that is surrounded by lava flows. Many birds and plants live in the kīpuka in Hawaiʻi Volcanoes National Park.

lūʻau (LOO-ow): A lūʻau is a traditional Hawaiian feast. You can go to a lūʻau if you visit Hawaiʻi.

maiʻa (my-ah): Maiʻa means banana in Hawaiian. You might pick a maiʻa from a tree in Hawaiʻi.

Mauna Loa (mau-nah low-ah): Mauna Loa means long mountain in Hawaiian. Climbing to the top of Mauna Loa is hard work.

mele (meh-lay): Mele means song in Hawaiian. Polynesians of Hawaiʻi told their stories through mele.

puaʻa (poo-ah-ah): Puaʻa means pig in Hawaiian. At a lūʻau, you will eat puaʻa.

TO FIND OUT MORE

⋀

FURTHER READING

Decker, Barbara.
*Hawaii Volcanoes National Park:
Fire from Beneath the Sea.*
Sierra Press, 2007.

Gill, Maria.
DK findout! Volcanoes.
New York, NY: DK Publishing, 2016.

Meinking, Mary.
What's Great About Hawaii?
Minneapolis, MN: Lerner Publications, 2016.

ON THE WEB

Visit our home page for lots of links about Hawaiʻi Volcanoes National Park:

childsworld.com/links

Note to Parents, Teachers, and Librarians:
*We routinely check our Web links to make sure they're safe, active sites—
so encourage your readers to check them out!*

INDEX

ABOUT THE AUTHORS
Teri and Bob Temple have devoted much of their adult lives to helping children. Teri spent 15 years as an elementary school teacher, and Bob has helped to create hundreds of books for young readers. Married for 20 years, the couple resides in Rosemount, Minnesota, with their three children.